Stories are written
to be told to
the very young and old


A Christmas Story

This is a work of fiction. Names, characters, places and incidents either are the product of the author's imagination or are used fictitiously, and any resemblance to any actual persons, living or dead, events, or locales is entirely coincidental.

Layout Designer: Ranilo Cabo

To order additional copies of this book, contact:
Xlibris
844-714-8691
www.Xlibris.com
Orders@Xlibris.com

| ISBN: | Softcover | 978-1-4257-8825-4 |
| --- | --- | --- |
| | Hardcover | 978-1-4363-1900-3 |
| | EBook | 978-1-5245-0519-6 |

Print information available on the last page

Rev. date: 11/14/2023

# PITTER PATTER VANCE

## The Dancing Unicorn of Tippy Top Mountain

## A Christmas Story

by Deborah Lane

Illustrated by Kevin Scott Collier

Way up the mountain at the very tip top of Tippy Top Mountain lived a family of unicorns and the oldest unicorn was Pitter Patter Vance. Vance did a dance upon the mountain everyday with his furry little friends. He was loved by all and loved to dance and sing. Vance was all black as the night with a purple mane of feathery soft flowing hair and had a beautiful horn of shiny gold he was always a happy fellow you see, he was the legend, the majestic one of all the unicorns in the forest of Tippy Top Mountain. All would follow him because he was the oldest unicorn the wisest of all, he new the way down the mountain to the town of elves and all the reindeers and that is where Santa lived. Someday he would take them all there and his furry little friends.

Mean while down in Santa's village, the big clock was ticking and time was running out, Santa was so sad; know one could help with the packing of all the presents for the big trip around the world to deliver gifts to all the children. The bells where ringing for everyone to gather for a meeting to pick someone to help. Ringgggg! .... ding-a-ling-ring! .... Ringgggg .... Ring—ding—a—ling while Santa was busy trying to gather everyone together he spied a shiny star bouncing and bouncing back and forth and up and down and all around above the mountain top of Tippy Top just a little in the sky below the clouds. Santa shouted! What is that? A shiny bouncing star!" Oh no, no no no! I know an elf yelled that is Pitter Patter Vance the very majestic wise unicorn, with the shiny gold horn! He must be doing his happy dance" he loves to dance with all the furry friends of the mountain. He does it every day said elf. Well! Santa said if he is such a happy fellow and majestic and wise maybe we can go and ask if he can help us. Oh right! … Said the elf sarcastically. Well I'm going Santa said, something has to be done about this sour problem we have. "Grumble" grumble" "grumble" he groaned! And off he went up the mountain all by himself.

No one even cared, they were tired and all self centered. A lazy bunch of elves and reindeers. They would not get anything for all the work they had done for all the children. They were sick of it year after year of giving there time and energy for nothing in return. How selfish the elves and reindeers had become poor Santa! And the children of the world. What was going to happen now?

Santa grumbled all the way up the mountain about how selfish they all were until he reached the top of Tippy Top Mountain. Santa stood there looking with surprise! It was so beautiful up there! The great trees green and lush with fragrance of pine and the holly bushes all around it looked like Christmas should look and there stood a beautiful unicorn he was black with a feathery purple mane and a horn of shiny gold! Santa was stunned with amazement why hasn't he ever met him. Or saw him, he thought. "Well-hello! Helloooo . . . ow! Said Vance the dancing unicorn. Santa stood amazed at his glory, just amazed finally answering Vance stuttering ya ah—h! Yes..-ss hello there! Are you Pitter Patter Vance the dancing unicorn said Santa. Well yes! "I am, and you must be the jolly fellow that I have heard about that delivers gifts to all the children around the world yes I am said Santa but I am not happy and jolly. Oh! Said Vance, what is the matter? I have a big problem in the village said Santa the elves have become lazy and selfish and Rudolph and the other reindeers have forgotten the power of giving and they just don't care about anything anymore. I need someone to help gather the gifts and pack and help me deliver the gifts the night before Christmas."

9

"One of the elves in our village told me about you. Can you help me? Well I don't see why not unless you have some sort of contract to sign or something you see I only give from my" heart and soul "because that is what I do, I give straight from my heart with kindness and sincerity that is what my family has taught me to do. Give straight from the heart and you will get the same in return. "Give!Give From your heart my parents always would say" and do that always and you will be happy that is why I am happy and every one knows who I am, Pitter Patter Vance the dancing unicorn on Tippy Top Mountain. I have to teach everyone the way. The way of the wise to be kind with sincerity, Vance said. Yes Santa I will help I will help from the bottom of my heart and soul. Thank you for asking me.

Vance asked all his furry friends of the mountain to help and they all agreed to go down Tippy Top Mountain to help. They all got in a line and danced there way down with Vance the majestic wise unicorn. Oh, what fun Santa was having with Vance and all the furry friends of the forrest going down the mountain. Singing and dancing all the way down.

(Song begins) ("singing")-—when you give the gift of kindness it inspires others too, to feel the gift of passion in everything you do. It's a wonderful feeling to do every day not just at Christmas just to have a special day. When you make someone happy it will always comfort you. The love that you give, will come back to you. So give a little kindness in everything you do it will make you feel happy and someone will feel special too! Oh there is so much fun in giving and helping the whole day through. It makes your heart beat happy just knowing we help you! There is so much fun in giving and sharing in the fun it will pay off in the long run when the love comes back to you!

As we go down the mountain singing, a song of joy we will make things happy for every girl and boy. Sing! Sing! Going down the mountain dancing all the way so much fun in giving is the only way. You can spread a lot of sunshine by giving kindness every day a little help to others lets you have a special day! (song ends) As they reached Santa's village closer and closer, the reindeers and Rudolph and the elves were all jealous of Pitter Patter Vance and the furry friends of Tippy Top Mountain top, calling them names and saying terrible things no one should say. Rudolph was all boosted out with comment. "Well well! Just look at them so proud of themselves! They think they are so special. Well! Just wait, you will feel like we do because we have been where you are going! Been there! Done that!, Ha!Ha!Ha!. Yeh! Shouted all the elves been there! Done that!

17

Pitter Patter Vance stood proud with all his majesty and said, "how terrible you all are! So smug with your voice of reticule! You all have lost the warm feeling of compassion and sincerity of giving kindness. The special moment when you have done all you can do to make someone feel special with love. When you give kindness, you receive a loving feeling back you know that! Said Pitter Patter Vance. Rudolph and all the elves just sunk with a horrible feeling of shame, for they had forgotten how wonderful they felt to give and especially the thrill of guiding the magical sleigh. There eyes teared up and they all sobbed. Oh! We feel terrible, just terrible. Said all the elves and Rudolph. We are so ashamed we are acting foolish we have forgotten all that. Will you help us? Asked Rudolph? Sure! Said Pitter Patter Vance that is what we are here to do. Lets hurry and get started, they all stopped crying and gathered together to help, and in no time at all with the help of each other, and no selfish remarks they managed to get the sleigh packed, and Santa was so proud and they were off on the journey of giving.

So when you see a shiny gold star along with Santa's sleigh Rudolph's nose is not the only one guiding the way. Just know its Pitter Patter Vance the dancing unicorn helping Santa in his own special way.

The End